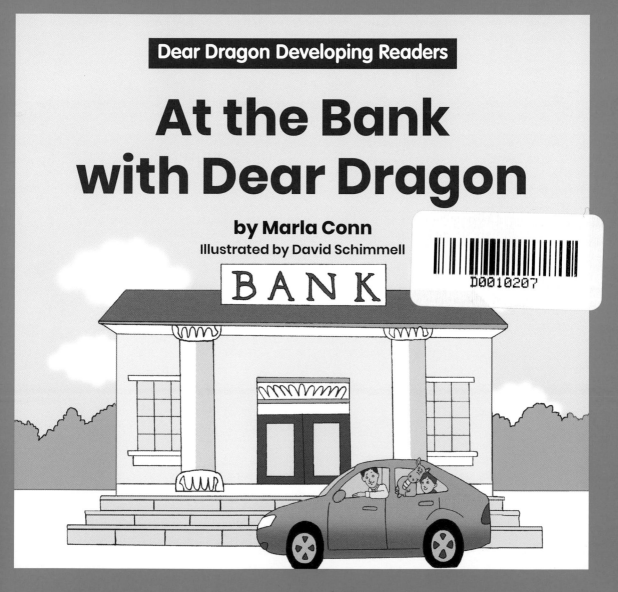

Dear Dragon Developing Readers

At the Bank with Dear Dragon

by Marla Conn
Illustrated by David Schimmell

BANK

NorwoodHouse Press

NOTE TO CAREGIVERS: It is a pleasure to have the opportunity to adapt Margaret Hillert's **Dear Dragon** books for emergent readers! Children will grow and learn to read independently with the boy and his loveable pet dragon as they have done for over 30 years!

The new *Dear Dragon Developing Readers* series gives young children experiences with book concepts and print, and enables them to learn how language works; phonological awareness, letter formation, spaces, words, directionality and oral and written communication.

Emergent Readers are just beginning to control early reading behaviors and require books that have a high level of support including:

- Predictable & repeated language patterns
- Simple story lines
- Familiar topics & vocabulary

- Repetitive words and phrases
- Easy high frequency and decodable words
- Illustrations that support the text

We look forward to watching the lightbulb go on as emerging readers expand their literacy powers; building important strategies for maintaining fluency, correcting error, problem solving new words, and reading and writing for comprehension. The *Dear Dragon Developing Readers* will ultimately guide children through the more complex text in *Dear Dragon Beginning-to-Read Books* as they become curious, confident, independent learners.

Happy Reading!

Marla Conn, MS Ed.
Literacy Consultant/Author

Norwood House Press
Chicago, Illinois

For more information about Norwood House Press please visit our website at: www.norwoodhousepress.com or call 866-565-2900.

LIBRARY OF CONGRESS CATALOGING-IN-PUBLICATION DATA
Names: Conn, Marla, author. | Schimmell, David, illustrator.
Title: At the bank with Dear Dragon / by Marla Conn ; illustrated by David Schimmell.
Description: Chicago, Illinois : Norwood House Press, [2019] | Series: Dear Dragon developing readers | Includes note to caregivers and activities.
Identifiers: LCCN 2018054633 | ISBN 9781684509966 (library edition : alk.paper) | ISBN 9781684043095 (pbk.) | ISBN 9781684043347 (ebook)
Subjects: LCSH: Readers (Primary) | Dragons—Juvenile fiction. | Banks and banking—Juvenile fiction.
Classification: LCC PE1119 .C6353 2019 | DDC 428.6/2—dc23
LC record available at https://lccn.loc.gov/2018054633

Hardcover ISBN: 978-1-68450-996-6   Paperback ISBN: 978-1-68404-309-5
319N—072019

Manufactured in the United States of America in North Mankato, Minnesota.

WORDS IN THIS BOOK

PICTURE GLOSSARY:

 money

 bank book

 bag

 piggy bank

 bank

 Dear Dragon

COMMON SIGHT WORDS:

- a
- at
- away
- big
- bring
- broken
- can
- do
- for
- good
- have
- I
- in
- is
- keep
- know
- like
- look(s)
- my
- new
- not
- now
- oh, no!
- place
- put
- that
- the
- this
- to
- we
- what
- will
- with
- worry
- you
- your

Oh, no!

Look at this.

My piggy bank is broken.

What can I do with a broken piggy bank, Dear Dragon?
What can I do with my money?

Do not worry.

We can put the money in a bag.

I know a good place to keep
your money!

We can bring the money to a big bank.

This is the bank.

The bank will keep your money for you.

The bank can put the money away.

Now that your money is in the bank, you can keep this bank book.

DATE	WITHDRAWALS	DEPOSIT	BALANCE	
06/11/12		$3.59	$3	59

Look!

A new piggy bank!

I can have money in the big bank and in a piggy bank that looks like Dear Dragon!

Word Work

Making New Words!

1. Write the word "bank" on a piece of paper.

2. Circle the letter that makes the "b" sound.

3. Circle the cluster that makes the "ank" sound.

4. Blend the sounds together.
   "b" + "ank" = "bank"

5. Change the first letter to make a new word. Try some consonant blends too, such as "bl," "fr," or "cr."

Activity

1. Collect several coins from home or school.

2. Place the coins in a bag for safe keeping.

3. Using a sheet of blank paper, fold the paper into fourths.

4. Sort the coins and count how many you have.

About the Author

Marla Conn has been an educator and literacy specialist for over 30 years. Witnessing the amazing moment when the "lightbulb goes on" as young children process print and learn how to read independently inspired a passion for creating books that support aspiring readers. She has a strong belief that all children love stories and have a natural curiosity for books. Marla enjoys reading, writing, playing with her 2 golden doodles and spending time with family and friends.

About the Illustrator

David Schimmell served as a professional firefighter for 23 years before hanging up his boots and helmet to devote himself to working as an illustrator of children's books. David has happily created illustrations for the Dear Dragon books as well as the artwork for educational and retail book projects. Born and raised in Evansville, Indiana, he lives there today with his wife and family.